JUST ME AND MY LITTLE BROTHER

BY
MERCER MAYER

For Arden and Benjamin
with love

A GOLDEN BOOK • NEW YORK
Western Publishing Company, Inc., Racine, Wisconsin 53404

© 1991 Mercer Mayer. Little Critter® is a trademark of Mercer Mayer. All rights reserved. Printed in the U.S.A. No part of this book may be reproduced or copied in any form without written permission from the publisher. All other trademarks are the property of Western Publishing Company, Inc. Library of Congress Catalog Card Number: 90-84584. ISBN: 0-307-12628-5/ISBN: 0-307-62628-8 (lib. bdg.)   A MCMXCI

We will do everything together,
just me and my little brother.
We will go to the orchard to pick apples,
and I will help him climb up.

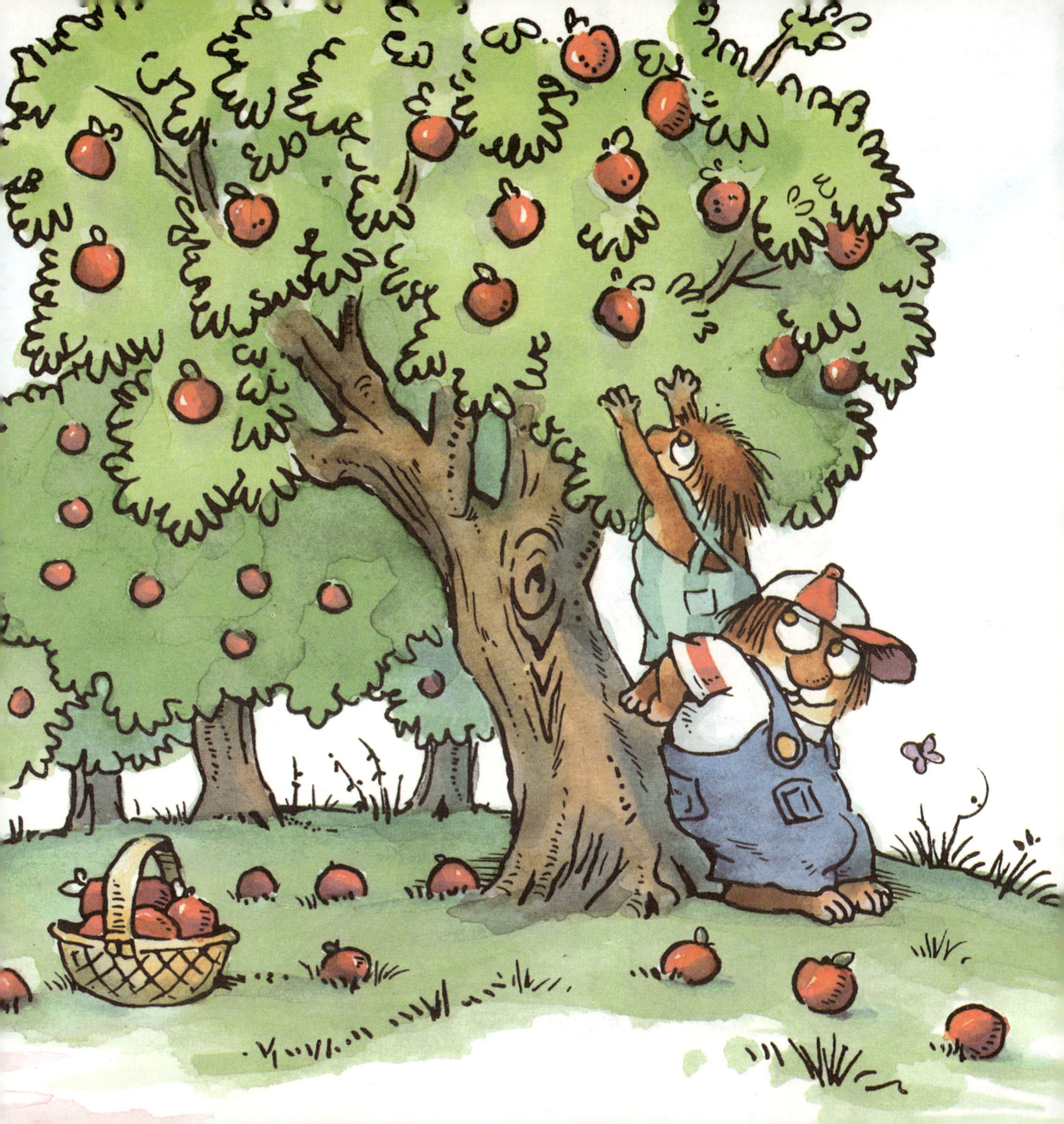

We will have bunk beds,
and I will have the top
'cause I'm bigger.

We can play space wars.

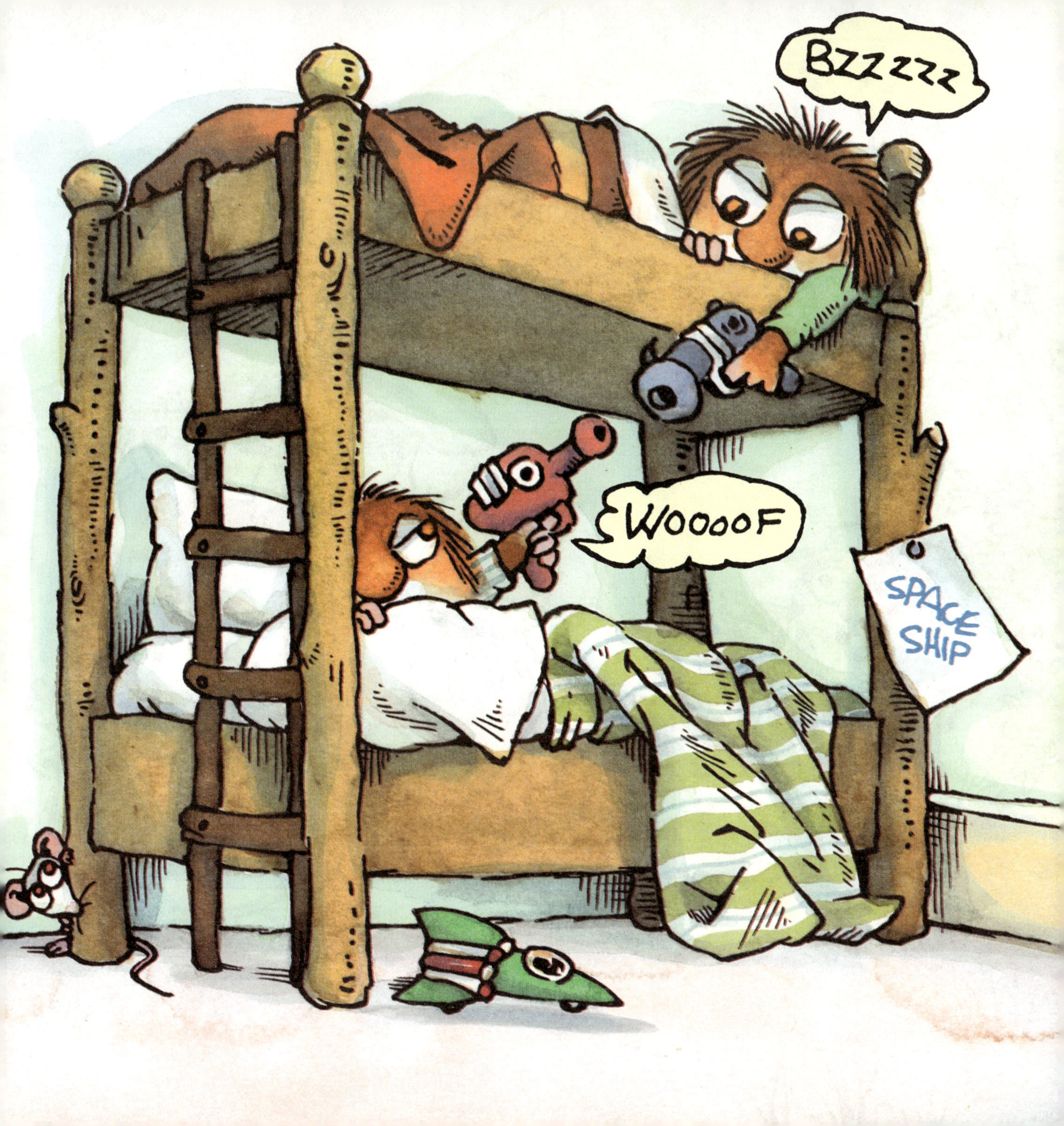

BZZzzzz
WOOOOF
SPACE SHIP

We will be real tough,
just me and my little brother.

The bully will run away when we come around.

We will stay up late and watch
the spooky shows on TV,
just me and my little brother.

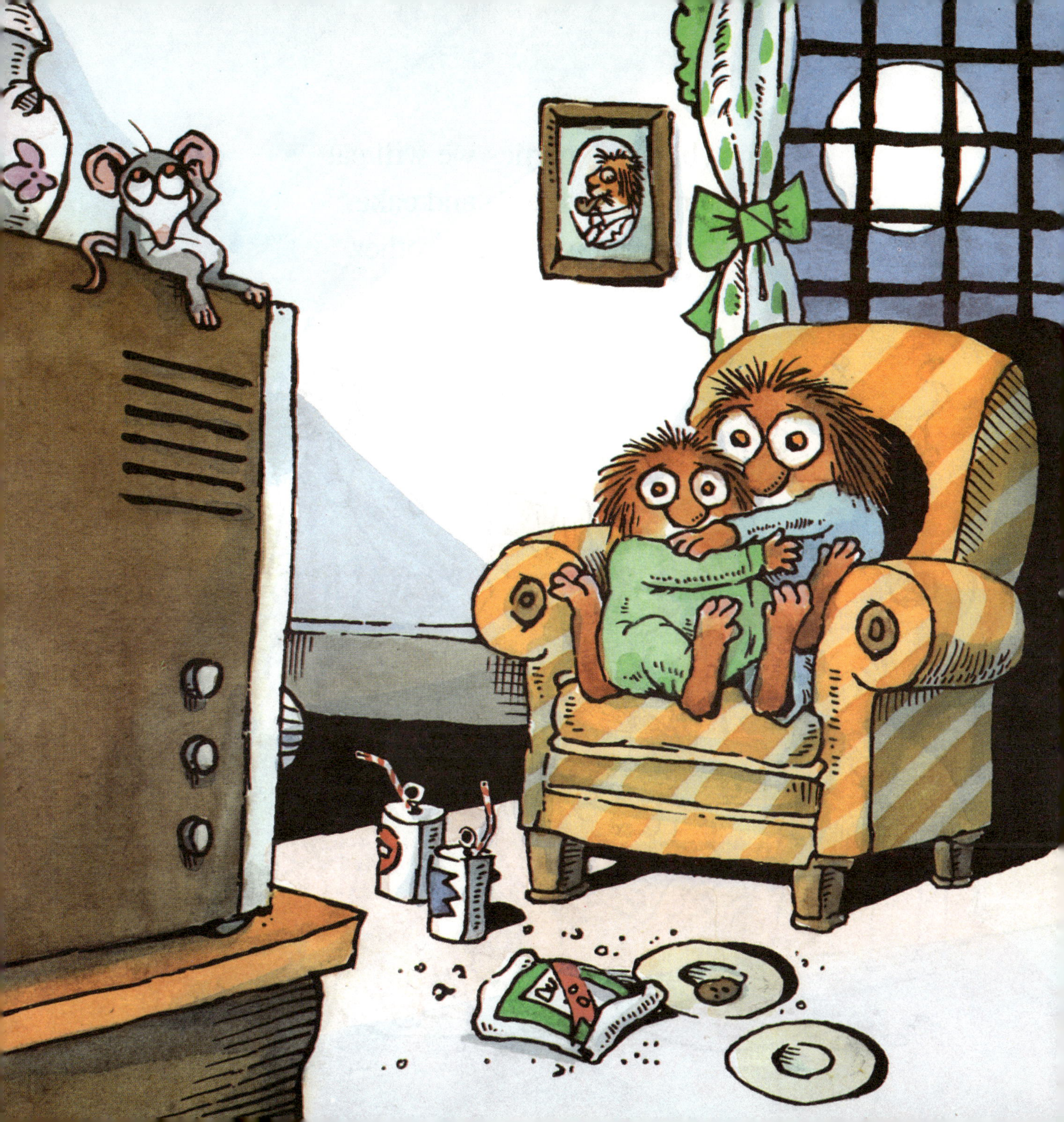

At birthday parties we will eat
the most ice cream and cake,
just me and my little brother.

We can play cowboys and Indians,
and I'll let him catch me.

On Halloween we can go trick-or-treating together, just me and my little brother.

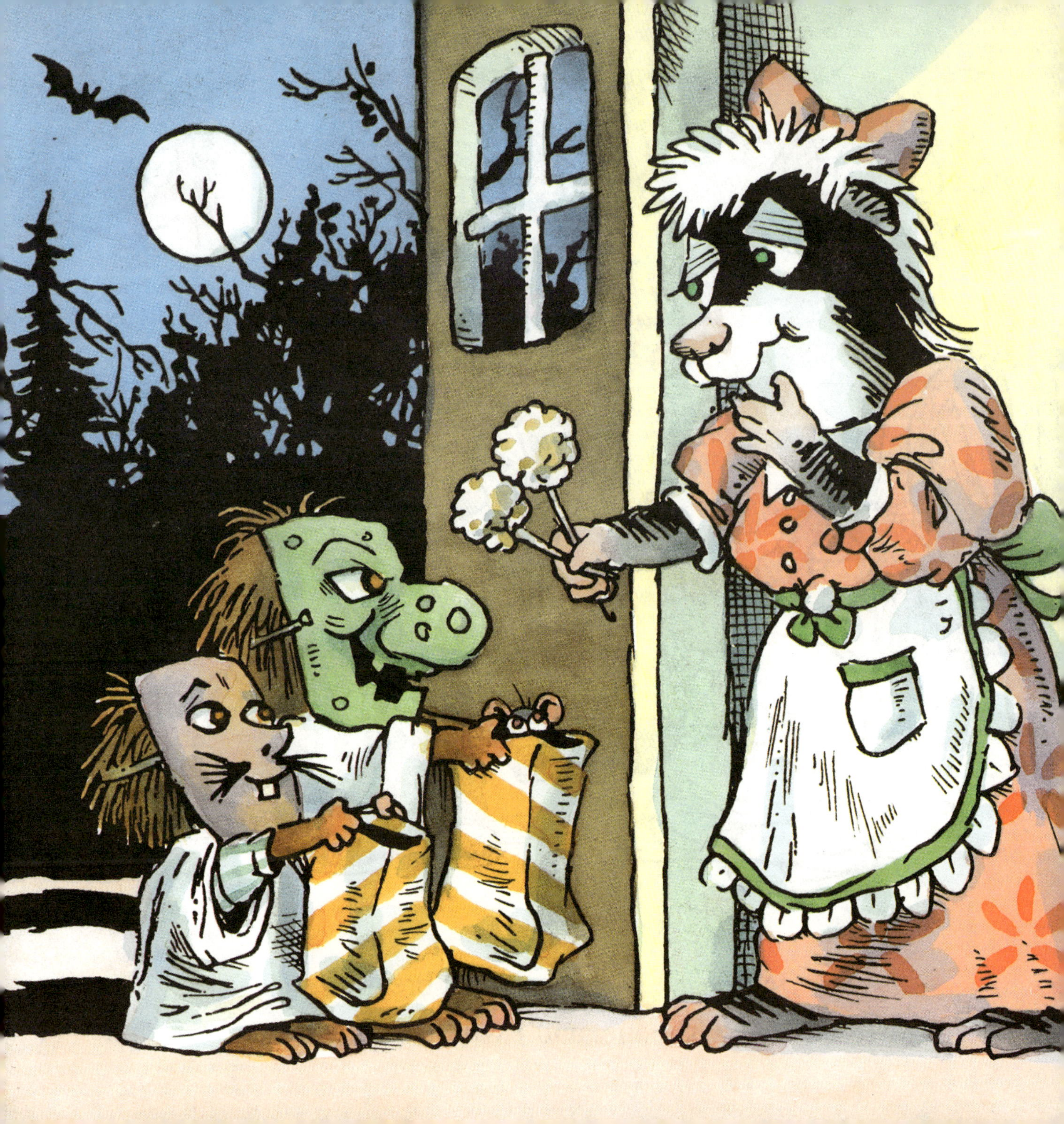

At Thanksgiving we will break
the wishbone, and I will let him win.

In the winter we will build a snowman.

We will build a snow fort
and have snowball fights.
Just me and my little brother
will be on the same side.

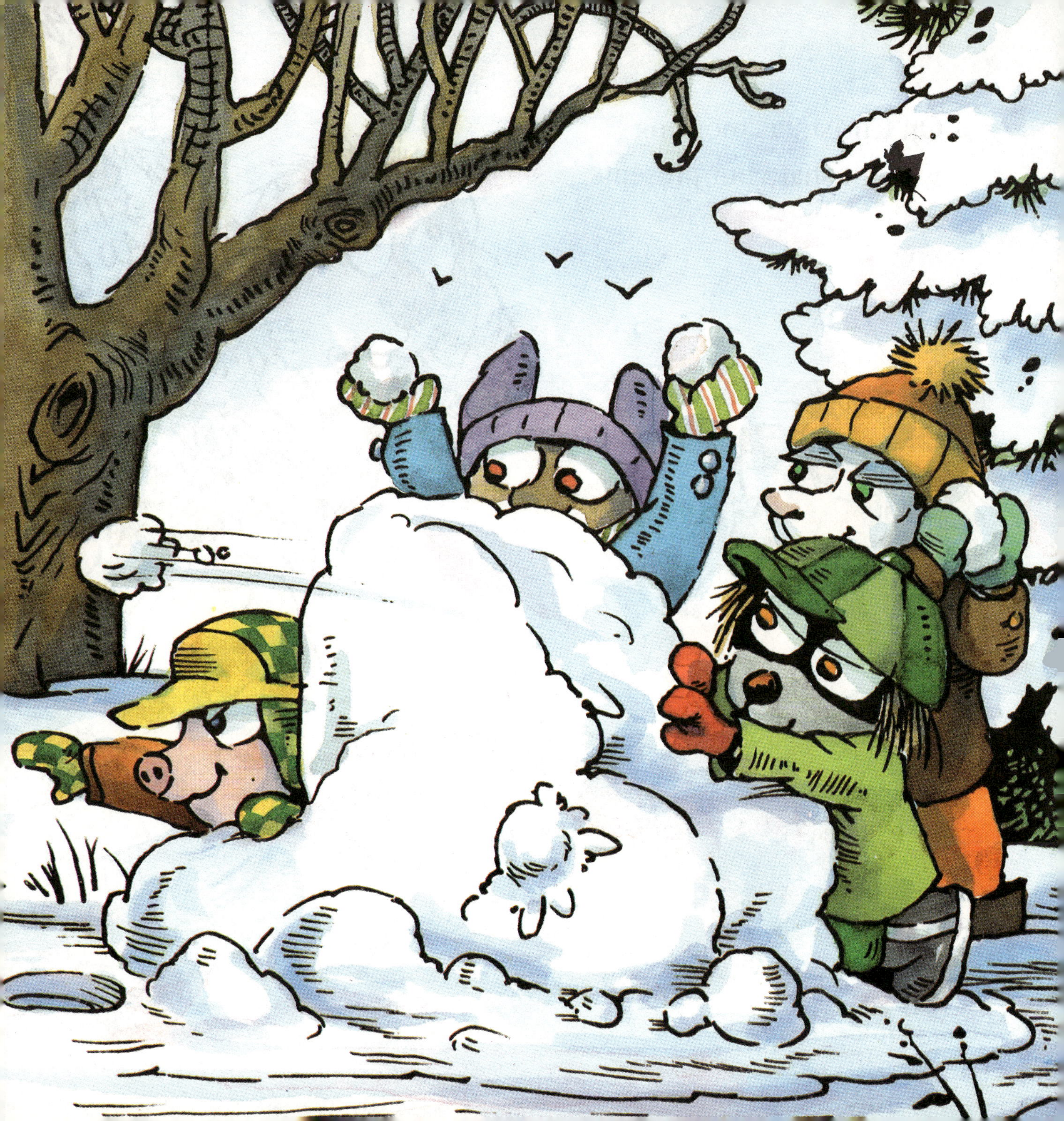

On Christmas morning
we will share our presents.

At Easter time we will hunt eggs together,
just me and my little brother.
And if he finds the most eggs,
I won't mind.

I will teach my little brother
to ride his bicycle.

He will have to practice a while.

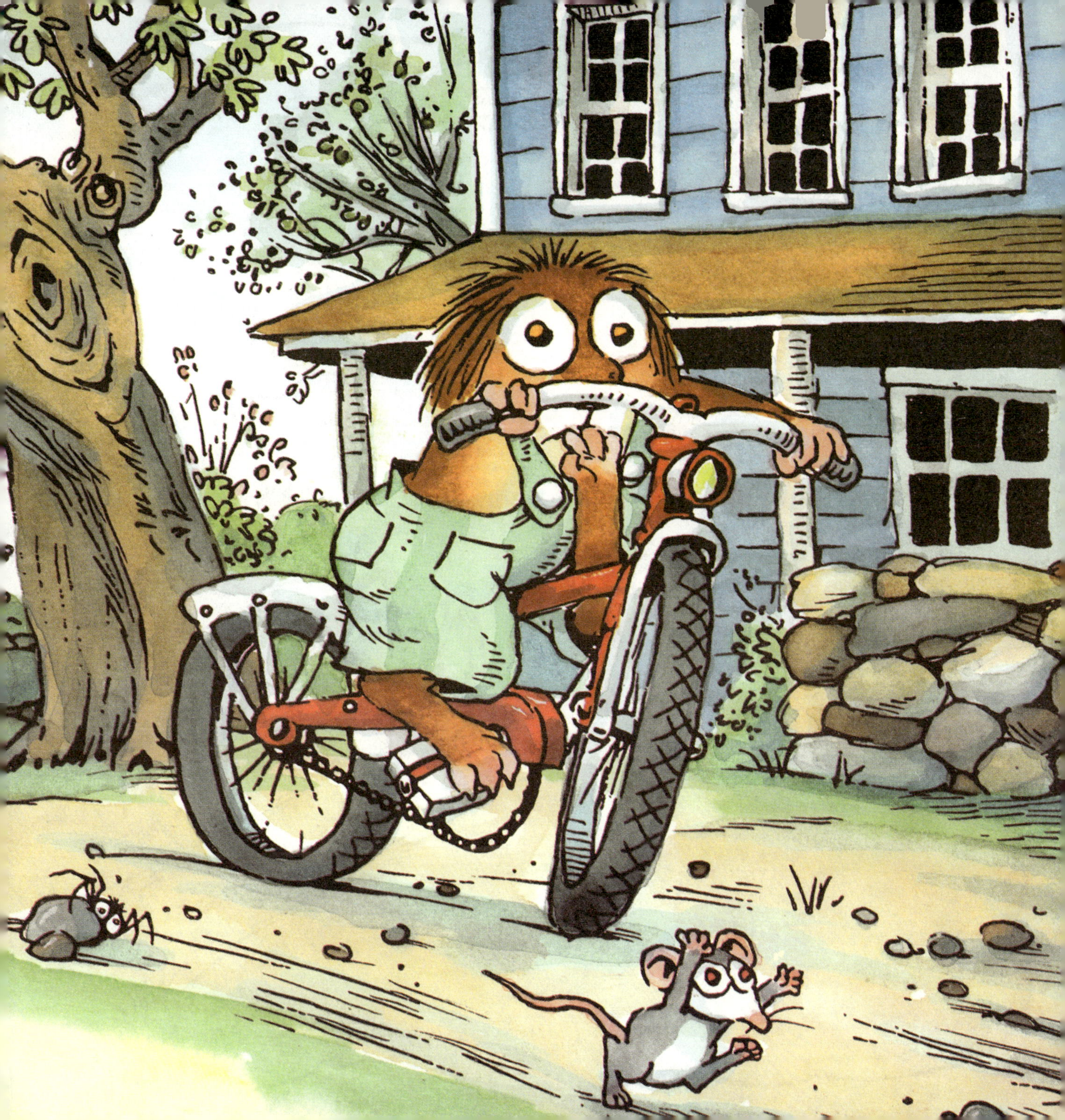

We will play all day
and never get tired.

There are so many
things we can do,
just me and my little brother.

But first he'll have to learn how to walk.